Tales of Ghosts, Woe, Warriors, Wolves, and Wind

Tales of Ghosts, Woe, Warriors, Wolves, and Wind
© 2007

Table of Contents

978-0-6152-0500-7

Tale 1. Ghosts of Teenage Fear

The words in the history book were beginning to blur. He needed to study for the test, to stay awake, but his head soon sank onto the open book. His face pressed against the print on the page and he was sleeping.

D'Icea was tall in life. She towered over him in death. The white trails of the mist inseparable from her slender strong form. His neck ached staring up at her, mouth agape.

"Have you come to seek revenge?" he asked the ghost, his voice wavering in the moist night air.

"It is not I who seeks revenge," said D'Icea. "T'irn, 80,753 lost. 100,073 mourn their passing. And you think I would seek revenge on one soldier."

"There are more who mourn your passing," said T'irn kneeling in the wet earth in front of her ghost. "They will mourn you for centuries."

"Does that change anything?" asked D'Icea.

T'irn stood and turned abruptly facing the man who rushed at him with a short sword drawn. Dodging beneath the swing of the blade T'irn stabbed at the man with his shorter sword. The sharp tip ripped into the man's clothing but laid not a scratch on the man's skin. The man turned towards T'irn sweat on his brow beneath his long light brown hair.

"You poisoned her!" he said, keeping his sword raised. The scratches of years of use in battle marred the blade and his own weatherworn face on the left side. "We could have fought our way to safety but you took it into your own hands."

"There were too many of them, A'il," said T'irn. "Would you rather they had taken her captive."

"You survived!" The accusing tone in A'il's voice was too much. They charged and fought with sparks flying in between their blades.

A'il was the stronger but T'irn had fought in more battles. He wove his shorter sword inside A'il's guard pressing forward to keep A'il's body in range of his blade. A'il struggled to bring his greater sword to cleave T'irn's body, blocking attack after attack with the guard and the base of his longer blade. T'irn drew his knife and lunged forcing the blade into the hide that protected A'il's body. A'il turned his body allowing the knife to rip through the hides causing nothing more than a scratch across his ribs.

Bringing the pommel of his sword down suddenly he struck T'irn on the head, the pointed hilt drawing blood from T'irn's skull. Knees weakened. T'irn fell. His shorter sword lay across the flattened grass and mud where they fought. His face held the pallor of death.

"I am sorry, D'Icea," he said. "Sorry, I poisoned you."

"And you were worried that I would seek revenge," said D'Icea sadly. "In life I held grudges. In death I understand life is greater than revenge. In life I might have been pleased with A'il. Today I am not."

A'il stood mouth agape in awe of the ghost of D'Icea that he now perceived after striking down T'irn. He fell to his knees. Then slowly he waved his hand through the mist of D'Icea's ghost. His fingers frosted over with tiny ice crystals when he held his hand within the mist.

"You are not real," he said in disbelief. "There are no ghosts."

"She is not real." T'irn laughed, coughed, and died.

A'il took his sword. He drew it across the ground away from T'irn's stiffening fingers placing it among his own weapons warming his frosted fingers against his own chest. He ignored D'Icea. Searching the corpse he took what coins were on T'irn's body and when he was finished he stood and walked directly through the misty form of D'Icea.

"You are avenged," he said, not turning his head towards the ghost but keeping his gaze set ahead in the direction he walked.

D'Icea appeared again in front of him blocking his path.

He walked through her a second time and then a third. The mist dissipating and then renewing her image each time he passed through. She held out her hand the third time and he stopped in front of her palm. He brought his own hand up and touched the mist of the palm allowing the frost to gather on the skin of his hand until there were distinct tiny rods of ice crystals.

"I did not desire his death," said D'Icea.

A'il stared at her image for a long moment and then he spoke. Behind him mist entered T'irn's corpse, swirled, and converged. T'irn's image stood beside the frigid body.

"You loved him," A'il said making the leap between the gap of memories from the battle campaigns and her strange behavior in ghostly form, his own face stretched taut in disbelieving shock.

"That is so," said D'Icea. "As I love you. But what you have done means I must now put up with his irritating presence for eternity."

T'irn's ghost appeared beside her own, his smile greater than it had ever been in life. A'il winced. His own hand fell away from the ghostly cool hand of D'Icea. The toes inside his boots received a great deal of his attention and then he smiled in a crooked fashion. His head raised again to regard the ghost of D'Icea.

"Have a good time in hell."

D'Icea laughed. "You two really did not get along. Did you?"

A'il laughed and spit past his right boot. "We were too busy fighting over you. And his battle plans just plain sucked. And by the way just because he is in hell I am going to go find one of those new priests and get myself a place in heaven."

"You don't think you will make it to Valhalla?"

"Hmmm," said A'il outloud. "So far I have killed a poisoner of warrior maidens and a bunch of cowards who wear armor and hide behind big shields. Nope. Give me a troll. Give me a dragon. Then I will crash the party in Valhalla."

D'Icea laughed again her misty form trembling with her mirth. "I'll not forget you. A'il."

"Wish I could forget you," said A'il. "Maybe I will go to hell for no other reason then to beat that smile off T'irn's ugly snout."

"Come join us ghosts," said T'irn. "I'll be waiting."

"Not yet," said D'Icea. "I have a task for you A'il."

"And what would that be?" A'il loosened the blade he had sheathed.

"Care for T'irn's family since you have deprived his children of their father."

A'il took his hand away from his sword. He twitched, shifting his weight to his left leg and then to the other. Finally he whipped his head up at D'Icea's image.

"Hell, NO!"

"Come now," said D'Icea laughing. "If anything could get you into Valhalla, taking care of any of T'irn's offspring should do it."

"D'Icea," said A'il. "First of all you are not real so I do not have to take orders from you anymore. Secondly any kids of T'irns are likely to invite Loki over for dinner seven times a week and they are more likely to think of me as Grendel than a replacement for their father."

"Just a thought," said D'Icea fading into the night, T'irn's ghost was no longer present.

A'il paused digging the side of his boot into the mud. "I've killed hundreds of men who probably all have families and you get all sensitive about T'irn's. Why his family?"

The mist reformed in front of him creating the shape of a small boy. The boy's clothes were tattered rags. He stared at A'il and reached out a hand, fingers curved over save for the finger near the thumb. A'il's own arm fell forward, his finger reaching to touch the ghost boy's. The pleading dullness in the boy's white expression caused A'il to step forward and then the image was gone.

A'il brought his head back seeking the stars above. Bright shining in the black sky. Then he ran.

West, north, east, south each held the form of a ghostly family in rags begging for bread. His boots froze in the rapidly chilling air and the hair raised on his arms. Cottages of mist went up in white flames. He nearly fell into the ditch trying to avoid the apparition with the soldier on the horse. His boots slid in the mud coming to a sudden halt he realized he had no idea where he was going. He bowed his head, a gruff laugh followed, and he stood in the midst of the mist.

"Tell me how to get out of here. " He said lifting his head. "And I'll do as you ask."

Light swirled and separated into glowing spheres lining a path through the darkness. He walked the middle path below the lights and his body warmed with the illumination of the sun's rays showing forth from below the horizon.

"You know I do not believe in ghosts," he said into the warm silence.

"That is alright," said D'Icea shimmering behind him in the air one last time before her image dissipated into the air. "We do not believe in you."

He woke with a start flinging the covers of his bed aside and displacing two history books. His hand went to the drops of sweat on his brow. His cellphone rang. After several moments of searching under a pile of clothes on the floor he snapped it open and listened to the voice speaking.

"History test. You said to call so you do not flunk like you flunked your English test 'cause you did not show."

"Yeah," he said. "I had a really weird dream."

"Yeah, . . . so you dating the Dacia chic?"

"No way. No way that I'm going to ask her on a date after that nightmare," he said. "I'm just not ready for…commitment and you know asking her out would be…and you ask her out and then the next day she moves in with you and then before you know it you have a family to take care of…and I just ain't doing it."

Tale 2. The Passing Autumn

"A person could get sick of this," said Sedy staring vacantly around the room where the dead carcasses of soldiers and family lay without movement.

The empty room did not answer her and she studied the dust on the floorboards her sword weighing heavy in her hand. Blue tunic and brown trews led to mud covered boots. She had a long lean body that Hivar examined from his hiding spot within the cupboard holding his last dart ready to shoot. Who knew how many more there were that remained alive and ready to kill her? And she had already cleaned the blood from her own sword. He had shot six, her sword cleaved four, and his darts took two more that ran in from the outside. They were lying prostrate on the floorboards near his hiding place and after many long minutes of observation they had not moved. He thought them dead. His attention did not remain on their corpses, but his eyes lingered on her curves and the long black hair braided back down over her shoulders to touch the black sheath of the long sword she carried under the black gauntlet on her left hand keeping the tip of it an inch above the floorboards. He waited but there was no more movement in the room and the silence convinced him it was over. The creak of the door when he opened it sent an unpleasant tingle up his spine. She was not surprised when he stepped onto the floorboard and straightened.

This morning before dawn after saddling her horse there was a moment when she knew there was someone in the stable besides her own horse and the horses of the guests. The uneasy feeling stayed with her when she was called back into breakfast. Her family would not let her leave without saying goodbye.

Then she went up to her room, claiming to have forgotten the drinking mug made for her by the town tavernkeeper, (he had given it to her for her birthday during the Autumn Equinox last year). The view from the window in her room showed her horse wandering free around the yard. The dead man curled over in his own blood was half inside of the doorframe leading into the stable. Two men were fighting in the yard between the stables. Hand to hand they were a blur to watch. Never before had she observed a fight with that level of skill. It was Hivar. She did not have a doubt then. The other man died with a sickening snap of the neck.

Hivar. The man she remembered ending the fight at the tavern in town four days ago glanced up at her, staring down from the window after the man's death and then ran into the back of the Inn. Another guest had walked into her room that same minute trying to convince her to sell her horse. She disengaged herself from the conversation politely requesting that he leave and waited a minute after he left not wishing to frighten him. Her father had long ago forbidden her to draw her sword inside the Inn saying it scared the guests but the fight below in the yard made her think it was time for that age old rule to be broken. Drawing her sword she was halfway down the steps when she realized her entire family, who owned the Inn, the soldiers guarding their wealthiest guest, and the people staying in the rooms were on the boards of the floor, sitting hunched over in chairs, and fallen over the table, arrow shafts jutting out from their bodies, a few with swords partially drawn.... They were all dead.

"You are not sad," Hivar said placing the darts away among the gear he carried, no sword, his kind rarely used them and he was not trained to fight with the bulky weapons most preferred by those who walked the streets by day.

"They were my guardians," said Sedy. In the moments following the fight she had gone to each of her guardians but the breath of life was not in them, their bodies were empty flesh and bone that no longer contained who they once were. "Not my parents, though I regard them to be my family. My parents perished before I was born. They worked for the king. I was sent here and I do not weep over their death. They are in a better place. I still have to live in this world."

"Well spoken," said Hivar. Paint covered him from his hair line to his waist: green, black, brown red smears camouflaging his white skin and his hair was cut cleanly falling to the base of his skull in strands of blonde, red, black, and light blue. "Mine died working for the Assassin's Guild when I was four years old. I did not know them but I remember the song my mother used to sing."

Humming a few bars of the tune he then sang a few lyrics: "Wake up sleepy and watch the leaves fall. Sleep heals the soul but when one sleeps one misses the tides of the moon. Night closes softly and all is silence. Day comes swiftly and work passes away but the stars always stay. Take me away to a sand covered beach and never let me stay in the rotting streets. Let me hear your voice for you are my choice."

Hivar stepped uncertainly towards Sedy. "She sang that to my father when they were young."

Sedy shifted away from the assassin. "Did he take her away from the rotting streets?"

"No," said Hivar his hands rested lightly over the hilts of a few of the knives he carried in his belt but they did not remain there. "They were starving and they both fell prey to the Assassin's Guild. Easy money but they lost their lives and they almost lost mine."

"Yet you are an assassin," said Sedy. "Where does the evil end?"

Hivar coughed lightly. "I am sorry."

"Everyone I know told me that to become a warrior is done to protect people and for no other reason," said Sedy lifting her sword over two inches away from the floorboards. "They trained me to protect people from assassins like you."

"You are a soldier," said Hivar with a hopeless shrug from his thin shoulders. She placed both hands on the handle of the sword. "You were born with the power to choose. I was born in the Assassin's Guild. I was marked from birth. They can kill me no matter the distance with the breaking of a simple spell. Tell me, should I have chosen death? Is that not evil? To cancel my own life before I had a chance to live it? That was the choice given to me. I will die outside of the Assassin's Guild. Do you want me to? Do you have the courage to run that blade through me."

"You just saved my life," said Sedy, a hesitant air about a woman who had never before hesitated about anything in her life. "How can you ask me if I want to take yours?"

"You think I am evil," said Hivar. "I never even had a chance with you because you think I am evil. And I am. I do not deny it."

"No, Hivar," said Sedy softly, taking her second hand away from the smooth wooden polished handle of the sword. "You are not. Not all of you. You did not have to leave me alive. You could have killed me. I did not know you were hiding in there until the dart hit the second man. Not all of you is evil. Your actions are evil. You kill but so have I. The greatest of evil is in people's actions, in what we are sometimes forced to do. I do not blame you for what has happened."

"You should," said Hivar sliding his boot to the side over the floorboards creating a grating noise that unnerved Sedy.

"I know people who let evil dictate their lives. They are slaves to it and they do not even think of doing what is right, do you understand that in this profession I could become that way. I fight it always but there may come a day when I lose."

Sedy set down the sword with an uneasy clank. The sound of her boots on the floorboards was thunder to his ears in the silence. Her hands brushed over his back smearing the paint farther on his body and his arms came around her leaving paint on her tunic.

"You won't lose. I will be there with you."

"You think this. Here I am," he said, bitterly sarcastic. "Hiding behind my war paint. Hiding behind the mask I was taught to wear from birth."

"It is the season for masks," said Sedy. "Why shouldn't you be wearing yours? In this season it is not just people. Even the trees mask their life."

"You think there is still love of life in me?" he asked.

"Why not?" said Sedy. "You are human, are you not?"

The war paint greased her cheek but she did not pull away from him. Hivar found her mouth with his own and there was another minute without words. He stepped to the side, her body following his movement, so that they could both keep watch on the door that lay aside allowing the daylight to stream into the room.

Sedy stared over his shoulder at the corpses of her guardians. Sad is not a word until a single stab of pain pierces the soul. A tear fell from the outermost corner of her dark blue eye and she blinked any excess water away with both of her eyelids, black lashes flitting against his skin causing unwelcome movement to his own solitude. He kissed her at the base of her neck near the shoulder.

"Please, do not," he said. "If you come with me I cannot be what you need. My life belongs to the Guild. I cannot always be there for you."

"First you ask me to come," she whispered into his ear. "And then you tell me not too."

Hivar laughed grimly. "I know myself. I know I cannot be there for you. I will never be there for you. Any children we have risks being branded the same way I was. Do you want to bring a child into the world knowing this? Knowing the child's own father cannot protect the child? You can ask for the child but if you are dead the Guild might take that child. Do you understand? It is not just my life. It is not just your life. We are deciding the life of our child."

"Calm down." Said Sedy gently. "There is no child yet. You have not been with me yet and consider this. Is it more evil to bring a child into a corrupt world than not to give a child a chance to be born in the first place? My people believe that there is life after this. Should we deny a child life because the first life is corrupt when there is a second life that will not be? Hivar, I love you. Do you understand?"

"No," he laughed grimly. "I hate myself. To understand why someone else could love me is beyond me."

"Well, I do," said Sedy. "So shut up, get on the horse out back, and let's go."

"My kind of woman," laughed Hivar. "You never back down do you."

"No," said Sedy breaking away from him. "And you are going to hate me when we start arguing."

Hivar laughed bitterly. "With you I have a chance of winning. With the Guild I have to take orders."

"Do you ever tell them to go jump off a cliff," asked Sedy walking over, intent on lifting and sheathing her long sword.

Hivar offered his hand and when she placed the hilt of the sword into it he sheathed it himself. It was a kindness offered, not forced and a show of trust. The length of the blade made it hard to sheath when slung over a shoulder. Sedy did not normally wear the sheath there but generally tied it to the saddle on her horse to be drawn more readily.

Hivar grinned, white teeth showing through the black and green paint that was now smeared on Sedy's face too. "You can. They do not own you. Be my voice to them. That is something you can do."

"Will they try to kill me?" asked Sedy in a nonchalant manner pausing at the door and glancing outside for more assassins and wiping the paint off some of her face with the back of the gauntlet she had on one hand, the second gauntlet was missing since this morning.

"Like these men?" said Hivar gesturing to the dead assassins. "No. These assassins trespassed. They took a Guild assignment. In the city where I live no assassins are allowed to give a lower price in a bid for a contract then the Guild. Assassins that are not with the Guild operating in Guild territory die unexplained deaths."

"Who was their target?" asked Sedy.

"The merchant by the fireplace," said Hivar gesturing towards the corpse in rich furs and gold surrounded by dead soldiers. "He intended to buy a warehouse near the docks that a rival merchant wanted. The rival merchant offered a contract to the Guild for his death but then gave the contract to these men when they said they could do the job for less money."

"And the Guild sent you," said Sedy. "Just you? One

against so many men?"

Hivar smiled a little, he was not a man who boasted. "I was trained by the Guild. They were not."

"Hivar," she said. "What would you have done if their target was alive?"

Hivar shrugged. "Let him live. The Guild sent me after the assassins, not after the merchant. I was late. The man outside was more skilled than I expected him to be. I am sorry. It was not my intent that any of these people should die."

"The intent behind the action that is where good and evil are judged," said Sedy. "Aside from what you are ordered to do you say you have good intentions."

Hivar shook his head in astonishment. "You think that erases what I have done. These men are dead. Assassins have families too."

"Yes," said Sedy. "But you let people live when another man might have killed everyone. That is what separates you from these men. Their target was the merchant. Just the merchant yet my family is dead because they were assigned to kill this merchant."

Hivar walked into the doorway allowing his own body to warm up against hers relieved that he did not have to step to the side and keep away from a woman out of respect for old traditions. The winter frost was biting his skin from outside. Autumn snows had covered the ground this morning announcing the beginning of winter for this year. Hivar was not expecting the snows for another month and the chill in the air was a shock to his bare skin covered by nothing but body paint from waist up and belts holding various weapons. Sedy pulled her own cloak from the wooden peg on the wall and wrapped it around his body. He kissed her again. He should not have. He understood that from past experience. He was not watching outside. Another assassin could kill them where they stood but the heat was rising inside and he could not stop. It was Sedy who broke away and started for the black horse saddled in the backyard.

The man waiting behind the shed brought up his bow drawing it back index finger above the butt of the arrow, middle finger below he aimed it at her back between the straps of the sheath that now held her sword. He suddenly felt very drowsy and fell over never suspecting the dart buried in his throat. Hivar held the next dart ready waiting for Sedy to finish unslinging the sheathed sword and tying it to the saddle on her horse.

"What did you name him?" Hivar asked Sedy when she turned in response to the noise she heard from the bowman falling to the damp earth.

"Thunder," she replied and Hivar laughed again, there was nothing on earth that would ruin his moment of happiness,

even if Sedy died right now he would always know that
there was someone on this earth in this life that loved him,
and that knowledge was priceless; more precious than
anything he could have ever thought of to be of value in
this life or the next.

"You should have named him Lightning," said Hivar. "The
way he struck down the first assassin this morning. I almost
gave away my position. I almost laughed. You know you
will never have to worry about that horse being stolen."

"I know," Sedy grinned. "Are you coming?"

"Is it safe?" he matched her smile.

"Are you worried about the horse or more assassins?" she
asked.

"The horse," he said thinking he would not hesitate to kill
more assassins but how could he kill a horse that belonged
to his beloved. "Definitely the horse."

"Come slowly," said Sedy motioning for him to lift up his
empty hand. "Let him sniff you. When he has your scent I
think it will be tolerable for you to ride with me, but he has
to be used to you before you can ride. Can you ride?"

"A little," he admitted. "I am not so skilled as you. It is
silly. I know where the heart of a horse is. I know how to
bring a horse down with a single shot but I have never
ridden one. I have always gone on foot to keep from

alerting my targets. This will be a new experience for me."

"Slowly and warily," said Sedy taking his hand in her own and lifting it up for Thunder to sniff and keeping his hand away from the teeth of the horse. "He will bite if he thinks you have a carrot or an apple."

Hivar smiled. "I would bite when offered an apple too."

Sedy laughed thinking of an old fairytale she had heard concerning apples. "I'll make sure never to offer you an apple then."

Hivar grinned. "Think it is too late for that. Besides I do not want an apple. I want you."

Kissing her forehead softly her arm made a very sudden movement that dug into his ribs. Hivar broke away slowly trying not to startle the horse. The man behind him choked on the blood spilling from his mouth seeping down his chin. He dropped the knife in his hand.

Hivar followed the knife's long fall to the frosted muddy earth where a few sprouts of grass lay flattened in the contrasting landscape. Sedy yanked her knife from the man's lung pushing the dying man away from them both. Gurgling and spitting the blood away from his lips the man made a valiant effort to rise and then fell to the earth his limbs stiffening in death.

"May he live to watch the sunrise in the next life," said

Sedy. "May there be someone here to care for his family and those who love him."

Hivar knelt down before her and taking a small worn rag from his gear he wiped the knife clean of blood. He glanced up at her when he was finished letting the rag fall to the earth. His hands clasped hers. She watched him without moving, aware that there was something she had done that made him behave in this manner that she did not understand. She sheathed the knife carefully when he was done but he kept her free hand in his own.

"I have saved many lives," he said bringing her hand to his lips carefully. "No one has ever saved mine."

"You might be surprised," said Sedy with a small amount of laughter. "You should do some more reading of history and legends."

"I do not know how to read," said Hivar with a laugh. "It was not a necessary part of my education."

"I will teach you," said Sedy. "Come. They should let me do that since it could help you in your profession."

Hivar smiled grimly. "Knowledge at work for evil purposes."

Sedy laughed in agreement. "Maybe I won't teach you to read. It might be too much work."

"Anything you want," said Hivar kissing her again and when they broke away from one another they were both smiling.

Mounting the horse she brought her hand down and he accepted the guiding hand he used to help fling himself up onto the back of the saddle.

"Are you sure he does not bite?" asked Hivar when the horse shifted beneath them.

"I am sure he does," said Sedy with the tilted smile she saved for his brand of humor.

Settling his body against hers he decided he would trust the horse for her sake. Brushing the braid of her hair away from his face he kissed the back of her neck.

"You really believe you can marry me, an assassin?" he asked, bringing an arm around her waist and laying his head against her back that was now free of the sword sheath.

Sedy's hand passed back over his leg reassuring her that he was well seated before she began walking Thunder away from the closest place she substituted for a home for most of her life. The truth was that she was more at home sitting atop Thunder than she would ever be sitting in a chair listening to her guardians talk to her about duty or trudging through mud across a battle field.

"It would be evil not to," she said settling her body more firmly against his. "When you find love. Do not deny it."

"Yet," he said tightening his arms briefly around her. "If I ever hit you or force you, I am ordering you to leave me on that day. Do not think I am not capable of it. Do not ever think I am not dangerous."

"Everyone is dangerous." said Sedy kissing him before bringing the horse around. Hooves trod over the fallen leaves of autumn. They rode into the sunrise.

Tale 3. Silver Polished Black

HIS THOUGHTS:

The dark gray shaded sky was beginning to lighten at the edges. His blue eyes settled on the gravestone. He stared blankly at the words engraved there. Wind chilled his skin prickling the unshaven stubs that shadowed the lower half of his face, separating the loose shirt from his spine, and swirling the dried leaves past the gravestone over his boots. He placed the silver bullet on top of the stone, knelt to his knees, and set a hand over the grave. Orange, brown leaves cracked under his hand.

"Coleene," he said. Tears threatened to break over the wrinkles at the edges of his eyes. "It took me a day to get out of jail. I was too late."

The image of Coleene's green eyes framed by her red hair and shadowed by the light freckles on her face hovered in his memory brought home by the howl unleashed with the next falling of leaves from the barren trees above.

Fingers dug into the earth scraped by decaying leaves rejected by the trees. He tried not to think about it. The cold from the ground seeped into his knees through the thin brown pants he wore. Frosted air reached into his chest and shoved out from behind his teeth more ghostly white in the dim light than visible smoke. Pain veined through his body throttling his lungs taking hold of his breath and shoving it into his guts.

"Coleene," he said, his fingers bled, the callused skin severed by a sharp point beneath the leaves.

Ignoring the fresh blood leaking off his shivering skin onto the dried corpses of leaves below, he lifted the ice glazed knife left over the grave ten months ago on the night he had sworn his oath. Broken oath…. The black polish on the silver blade had worn thin; there was no wood set around the metal tang to serve in the way of a handle. Nothing but a poor wrapping of thin black leather straps to gentle the grip of the hilt. He turned his left empty palm towards the thunderclouds, drawing the long sleeve of his shirt back with the tip of the knife. Blood welled up from the fresh tears in his skin dropping to the leaves beneath. The glint of light on the edges of the blade from the full moon above pierced his mind sending tremors into his spine. Wind brushed the black hair against the back of his neck reminding him he should use his gun but there was no guarantee that death would end all of the pain. Setting the flat of the blade against his wrist he shut his eyes.

"Please, show me a way…" he said, but all he felt was the emptiness of the lone grave in the hollow of trees and the wind brushing up against his clothing and skin. The sun remained hidden behind the dark silhouette of mountains.

The noise of broken leaves crunching beneath a second pair of boots irritated his ears but he did not open his eyes. The soft skin of another hand opened his confiscating the knife and gently shutting his fingers over the blood. Arms wrapped around his shoulders and his forehead sank into a strong boned shoulder. The sobs that wracked his lungs left him weary and wroth with the lack of the stoic expression he had worn through all the years of disaster after disaster with no solution save to stay alive. His eyelids lifted to reveal a delicate pale face partly encircled by dark wavy strands of hair and deeper brown eyes glaring into his soul. He winced at that stare hand reflexively drawing the gun. Her hand was quicker, preventing the draw with soft pressure on his wrist. In her other hand was the silver knife. His vision focused on the black polish, muscles relaxing when he witnessed no rash, (the effect that warped the bare skin of the elders when they met with silver), on her arm from the metal of the blade. Nothing but pale skin beneath the bunched up sleeve of her shirt all the way down to the long fingers gripping the silver blacked hilt. She was not one. He did not have to shoot her. The growl that emanated from the trees left little doubt that he had been spotted by one of the less powerful younger ones.

The woman's eyes left his to stop ten feet away by the large wolf stalking out from beneath the trees. Stiffened fur underneath laid back ears and frosted blue eyes mirrored her shape above the snarl of fangs. She brought the knife up out of instinct but her other hand was moving toward the black handle of the gun strapped to her belt.

Grabbing her elbow he jerked her hand away from the handle of the gun and her shape away from the wolf. His own gun was in his hand but when he leveled it at the wolf the hand shook. Dawn shattered over the mountains. The first gleam of light from the sun struck the fur tips of the wolf. The tips shrank from the light. He shut his eyes from the glare pressing his hand over the woman's arm to keep her from drawing her gun, his own .45 sank to the ground. The water forced out of the seams in his eyelids. He felt the tension leave the woman's body and let go of her arm. His eyes opened to see the young girl laid out over the leaves beneath the trees in place of the wolf.

"She is my daughter," he said.

The woman dropped the knife, slid over to the girl, placed a hand over her forehead and two fingers on her neck. She looked back over her shoulder, eyes measuring his soul.

"She is still breathing."

HER THOUGHTS:

The night shadows were lightening into day. The trail she had lost five hours ago was not marked on the district map. She sighed. It was not that the work was beyond her abilities but she preferred to have a decent map. It simply was not fair to send her out at night after a rapist vampire without a decent map. She shrugged. At least, the night vision contacts worked. The trail had utterly vanished and four werewolves later she had no idea how to get back to the vehicles except to keep walking southwest, and that was a guess. She lifted the night vision contacts up staring at the moon. The werewolves had not been very helpful. In their wolf forms there was no talking to them. It was either shoot them or be their breakfast. She hated shooting them but after the community of bit human werewolves had voted on the county ballot to be shot rather than rehabilitated there was not much law enforcement could do about it. Most of the werewolves in the small community were firm believers in Christ, regularly attended church, and insisted they would prefer being sent to heaven to running the risk of eating another person. The government had assured the public over the news that scientists in secret government facilities had been working on the cure for the Lupine virus, (a virus turning people into werewolves), for two years and they were very close to finding an anti-virus to bring people back from wolf form. Everyone conveniently forgot that this same news was announced two years ago by the same president.

The animal rights activists and human activists had joined forces in an effort to make silver bullets illegal to own, but that proposal had been voted down very quickly. Random Native Americans and very animal friendly people had volunteered to be bit but that was discouraged by the local mayor and a very grisly report of the first humans to be massacred by the werewolf community had finally been released by the government to the press. She shook her head, thinking their energies might have been better spent hunting down the elder werewolves that were still biting people, but they had claimed diplomatic immunity. She sighed again reminding herself that it wasn't her job to worry about politics. Her job was to hunt down the vampire rapist and quietly shoot him with a sharp wooden bullet. Mission accomplished a little ash on the night air and nothing more. It probably wouldn't become a diplomatic incident, but if it did, then no one saw it. Her boss was planning on sending an anonymous message to reassure the family of the victims but it wouldn't be on the news. She felt sick about the last thought trying not to remember the pictures of the victims and her stride quickened a little until her eyes spotted a gray stone in the middle of the clearing up ahead. A marker? She looked down at the map wishing GPS worked in this area but there was nothing indicating any gray stone. Securing the map back inside her pocket she approached the clearing with caution and realized the stone was a marker. The marker of a grave.

The single silver bullet set atop the gravestone indicated that the man kneeling near the grave was a werewolf bounty hunter, not a werewolf but still she hesitated to walk into the clearing. The elders were able to stay in human shape at will, even during the full moon. At the edge of her sight she noted the gleam of moonlight reflected in the silver ring on the man's left ring finger reassuring her a second time that he was not a werewolf.

The rash that would occur on an elder's skin at the touch of silver was absent from the man's left hand. When she took the first few steps out from beneath the trees she did not immediately go to speak with the man, instead she paused to read the engraving on the gravestone.

Coleene Mark
Dec. 25, 4002
Beloved wife and mother
Gone on permanent
vacation.

The wind swirled through her dark hair and she smiled at the thought of someone thinking of heaven as a permanent vacation, but the knowledge that she would never meet this woman in this lifetime brought a great sadness to her soul. She turned to look on the man whose clothes were worn thin, lavished with dried leaves, mud, and holes.

The man did not look like a hardened criminal and his skin was too dark to be a vampire. Her eyes focused on the unshaven lower half of his face. Frosted air shoved out by his lungs through gritted teeth shown ghostly white in the dim light. Her mouth fell partially open at the sight of the knife he held against his bare wrist.

The blackening on the silver blade was worn thin; there was no polished wood set around the metal tang to serve in the way of a handle. The man's bloody fingers gripped the poor slender hilt. He turned his left empty palm skyward, drawing the long sleeve of his shirt back with the tip of the knife. The glint of light on the edges of the blade from the moon above pierced her soul. Wind brushed through his black hair leaving it unsettled against the back of his neck. He spoke but she did not hear the words he said. Stepping closer over the dried leaves the image of the single silver bullet sitting on the gravestone echoed in her mind. She knelt down beside him and confiscated the knife gently shutting his fingers. Wrapping her arms around his shoulders she thought of her nephew the day he had learned he was a werewolf. She thought of the day his father, (her brother), shot him and was sentenced to death by a court of law. A single unnoticed tear slipped down her cheek onto the dried leaves below. Then there was the day she had renewed her vows to the church and they had sent her out here to hunt a foreign vampire.

The man's hands clutched her arms causing bruises; sobs wracked his chest and tears soaked her long sleeved blue shirt. When his breathing slowed he looked into her eyes. His blue eyes were stunningly perfectly shaped. She wondered why it was always the eyes that struck her about a person first, never the nose, the hair, the shape of the mouth, or the wrinkles acquired through the years. His dark icy eyes were flooded with grief. He winced away from her hand, reflexively closing over his gun. She quickly placed her hand over his, preventing the draw with soft pressure on his wrist using the hold they had taught her back in her earlier days of training. The black pupils of his vivid blue eyes went to the knife she held in her other hand. She thought about reassuring him that she was no werewolf but his muscles relaxed before she could speak and the man's hand fell away from his gun. The growl that emanated from the trees behind her made her aware of the wolf stalking out from under the barren limbs of the trees.

Drawing her gaze away from the man's intriguing eyes she fixed her view on the large wolf. Stiffened fur underneath laid back ears and frosted blue eyes mirrored her image above the snarling fangs. She brought the knife up out of instinct but her other hand was moving toward the black handle of the gun strapped to her belt.

The man grabbed her elbow jerking her hand away from the handle of the gun and swinging her body off balance away from the wolf. His own gun was in his hand but when he leveled it at the wolf the hand shook.

Dawn shattered rays of sunlight over the mountains. The first gleam of light from the sun struck the tips of fur belonging to the wolf. The tips shrank from the light. The man shut his eyes from the glare pressing his hand over her arm to keep her from drawing her 9mm, his own .45 sank to the ground. She watched the wolf in amazement wondering whether this was the same way her nephew had shifted from wolf form into human, but the sight was gruesome. The sight of shrinking and altering of limbs twisted within her gut causing the breath to freeze in her lungs. The man let go of her arm. When the shift was finished a young girl lay over the frosted brown leaves beneath the stark trees in place of the large snarling wolf. "She is my daughter," The man said, the strangled note in his voice bit the chilled air.

Laying down the knife, she cautiously approached the werewolf girl thinking that perhaps the news report she had seen this morning about the success of the anti-lupine virus they had developed in Japan might possibly be true. She set a hand over the child's forehead and asked for a blessing and stretched out the two fingers of her other hand to search for a pulse. She looked back over her shoulder, at the man whose daughter was a werewolf and said.

"She is still breathing."

WHAT THE WOLF THOUGHT:

The smell of silver in the air itched. The sneeze was unexpected but it cleared the sinuses. The animal was near. Air let loose on the wind from the excitement of bounding down the mountain trail. Frosted leaves underneath provided a sliding ride into a soft bit of mud not yet frosted by the chilly air near the base of the trail. The passage of scents left behind was aggravating. There was a mouse running through the brush to the left but it was so small and it escaped in a hole beneath a tree. The ache of emptiness in the stomach was large. The wind shifted downward bringing with it the smell of pine needles buried beneath the leaves, but there was a much stronger scent to follow on the ground. Slower. The trees ended. Anger emanated from the lungs at the sight of two large animals instead of the one whose smell was on the trail closer to the earth.

Fear. Itchy. Anger. Not to eat would prolong the ache in the stomach, but there were two big animals, not one. The thought of the small mouse back on the trail flitted through the brain before the pain struck and seeped inward twisting organs and straining the breath from lungs no longer in their proper order to breathe. The leaves beneath were suddenly frozen and cold.

"She is my daughter." The echo of the voice in her ears was familiar but not the strangled tone.

Warm soft fingers rested above lidded eyes.

Mother? The thought leaked into the mind but the heaviness of sleep drapped over and into all of the senses bringing forth, for the first time, peace.

Tale 4. Save the Wind

The path was rough with brush, smooth rocks, and dust. Three people forged their way up walking between the rising rock on both sides of the path. The gap was wide. The path veered to the side of the solid reddened rock cliff. Two of the travelers were young boys. Rule was the youngest. He was a pale slender lad. His breath did not come easy on this long walk up hill. His hair was black and he walked slowly laboring to keep up with the older boy who ran ahead at times then circled back past the old man who was the third traveler. The older boy was a head taller than Rule. His skin was ruddy, hair brown, and his mouth was full of laughter. The old man, who carried a gnarled walking stick, called to the older boy often warning him not to run too far ahead. His patience was wearing thinner than his white hair. His beard was a narrow affair that dipped down from his chin but did not fall anywhere near the ground. His eyes were bright and keen in his leathery weathered face and hardened expression. There was not much laughter in his eyes and his nose drooped down from the weariness of all the years he had lived.

"Minut!" The old man called out to the oldest boy. "Stop running ahead or I will start throwing my stick out and ask you to fetch it the way I would speak to a dog. Cease this foolishness right now for we have a long way to go and you will soon need your energy."

Minut looked back at the old man and laughed. He replied with two short sharp barks. The old man shook his head and stopped to lean against a gnarled tree very near the wall. The branches of the tree brushed alongside the wall in places. The wind caused them to bend near the wall and the higher branches ran parallel to the smooth stone but this tree had lost every leaf long ago. There would be no new leaves until spring. The ground was littered with brown-orange withered leaves. Rule avoided the leaves, walking silently upon the path.

"Sage?" said Rule to the old man. "Why are there lines upon the cliff face?"

The old man looked up in the direction that Rule pointed. The youngest boy had finally caught up with the old man and stopped walking once he was beneath the tree. His short arm was uplifted and his pointing finger was extended upward to a place on the wall a full length of a man higher than the height of the bent over old man leaning against the tree. The Sage let out a huff of ragged air from his thin chest.

"Ah, but that is a wall, not a cliff and there are no lines on it," he coughed. "More likely to be shadows or indentations in the rock. Perhaps no more than our own imaginations, waste no thought on them, leave them alone. Minut! Come back here and stand still for a moment's rest and I will tell you all you need to know of life."

Minut ran back down to the tree and stood beside it flushing a grouse from the brush in a great thumping of flutter of wings. The old man shook his head. Minut smiled and laughed.

"Ah, Minut, you must leave the creatures alone," said the old man. "For they have a right to live lives, also. The person who takes the right from them has no right to complain when his peace is taken in return."

"Ah, Grandfather!" said Minut. "Have to have a little fun."

"Do you think it was fun for the grouse?" The old man eyed the eldest boy with a stern expression on his face.

"But how do you know it was not fun for the grouse?" asked Rule Ylliath.

Minut snickered. "Why does he talk so funny, Granddad?"

The Sage glared at Rule. "The result of reading too many books, I shouldn't wonder."

"Like you haven't?" said Minut. "You talk as funny as him."

"I am certain that I do," said the old man. "Now listen grandchild. There are three roads in life. The road leading to less, the middle road in between the first two roads, and the road to excess of which you know too much. Which of the three would you choose if you had a choice?"

Minut looked up at Sage and scratched the dry itch behind his left ear where a bug had landed a moment before. Rule stood still considering the question. Minut laughed.

"Who cares?" he said.

"Ah," said the old man in a tightly clipped tone of voice. "You might care in the future for the road to less leads to loneliness and the road to excess leads to insanity, therefore the middle path is best chosen."

"The middle path is boring," said Minut.

The old man snorted at the eldest grandson's reply. Then he turned his eyes to the younger grandson. He gestured for Rule to answer.

Rule tilted his head to the side in thought, then spoke quietly. "I don't think the middle path would be so boring if a person could fly it instead of walking."

The eldest son laughed at this reply. "Fly? Look at your back, brother, do you see any wings?"

Rule shrugged and looked at the ground. The old man rolled his eyes. Then he tapped the end of his stick in the dust, clearing his throat at the same time.

"I think you are both too young to understand life," he grunted, and pushed away from the tree, once again starting up the path on gnarled old legs. "We shall have this 'talk' again in the future. Hopefully, you will both be at the proper age to understand it."

Rule looked toward the old man, he looked at the tree, and then he looked at the lines upon the wall. Rule kept his eyes focused on the lines he saw on the cliff near the high branches of the gnarled tree. He thought the lines might be ancient writing. His limbs were weary with the dust of travel and the weight of his clothes. Still, he dreamed of climbing that tree and reading what was written.

Minut ran ahead now that the old man was finished speaking. He thought the speech a simple delay for the old man to catch his breath. "Busy work" adults assigned to kids when the adults could not keep up.

Rule set his eyes on the lowest branch of the tree and he set his fingers and toes to the trunk, he started to climb. He swung his right leg over the lowest branch when the old man turned his head back to see what was keeping his youngest ward.

"Rule!" The old man said with a hard loud tone. "Stop wasting daylight with your foolishness! Jump down and hurry up about it. Old tree will probably break under the weight of you. Down with you! Stop wasting my time!"

Rule looked at the lines he was sure were more than shadows of his imagination. There were small cuts in his hands where he had scraped them against the trunk of the tree. He looked back at the old man.

"I want to see the lines on the wall," said Rule. "I can't fly, so I climb. I want to see what they are. Maybe someone left them there for us to find on purpose!"

The lines were becoming visible. Rule could almost trace them with his fingers but he could not touch the words. The lines went back and forth thus:

For God so loved the world that he gave his one and only son that whoever believes in him shall not perish but have eternal life. For God did not send his son into the world to condemn the world but to save it.

Jn. 3:16, 17

The old man grunted and tapped his walking stick against the path. "And maybe you have nothing but sticks for brains. Get down here, boy! We have a long way to go."

Rule glanced at the lines then let loose of the tree branch sliding painfully down the trunk until his feet struck the ground and he felt the force in the jarring of his knees. He glanced up the wall and wondered where the lines had come from and whether they were chiseled into the wall or someone had used paint to place them there or charcoal. He was certain they were not shadows in the cliff. There was a lingering idea beneath the shallower thoughts spinning in his mind that those lines were important for a reason he could not explain. The Sage called to him again. Rule looked away from the wall and set his foot to the small path. Walking dutifully after the old man Rule left the tree to the bird that winged in from the sky and perched upon the branch near the lines on the wall. The youngest boy soon left it far behind on his way up the small path in accordance with the old man's command.

The bird perched on the branch oblivious to the travelers who had stood below. The bird was not interested in the lines on the wall. Birds knew what it meant without ever having to read it, but the people did not. Wind blew through the canyon over the small path below. The tip of the bird's beak tapped on the middle line on the wall. Might be he was unbalanced by the wind rocking the branches of the tree and the tap of the beak was a simple correction of balance. The wall gave way beneath the bird's touch disrupting the bird's perch on the branch. The bird took flight off the branch of the tree. The wall gave way and a door opened, but no one was there to enter…save the wind.

Tale 5. The River Troll and the Knight

The sunlight was shattered by the dark tree limbs rising above the dying warrior's helm, the sunrays rested around his still form. Hand pressed against the wound, he kept the blood from seeping out between the chinks in his black plate armor and falling to the dark green grass. He raised his head at the smallest sound. The whistle on the wind was followed by a small twig snapping beneath the smallest boot he had seen since walking on the city streets of Beren. Before him was a short person he thought to be a child. Dressed in a well made jacket, tunic, pants, and an array of belts made from what appeared to be the discarded shed skin of the Sabercats that roamed the mountains, she stood no higher than the bottom of his chest plate. He thought someone so small and slight might have run from him at his full height but he was not standing now. Laid out on the ground with the weight of a dead Grear carcass over his knees he was not intimidating.

The dark mustache that ran down in straight lines on either side of his chin was wet with perspiration and dark specks of blood from the spiked Grear. Razor sharp fins jutted from his own black plate armor in imitation of the Grear hide and scales.

"When in the Grear Mountains," he muttered remembering why he risked his own life by wearing sharp armor. "Have a hide stronger than a Grear."

"I am not a Grear," said the child, her ears were narrow and keen.

"So you are not," he said shoving at the corpse stuck fast over the plated armor on his legs with a black scaled gauntlet, but there was no strength left in his arm to move the metallic blackened carcass. "Unless you are a healer this pack of Grears have ended my life. But you do not carry the staff of a healer or am I wrong again?"

"Not a healer," she said then whistled into the wind. "But I've a message for Var Al'keel of the Stone Keep. Are you Var Al'keel of the Stone Keep?"

"Was," said Var Al' keel holding up his right hand dark red with his own blood. "In a few moments you can say I was Var Al'keel."

"That won't do," she said whistling into the wind a second time with a long series of sounds ending on the lower range of musical notes. "I have a message to deliver to you so you cannot die. You'll just have to stay alive until I am done reading this."

Sitting down abruptly beside him on the grassy hill beneath the shadows of the tree limbs, she took out a small letter from her satchel made of shed Sabertooth hide. After showing him the letter she opened it when he tapped the wax seal with the metal gauntlet. The scrape of plate metal against plate metal made an odd sound in the silence hanging heavily over the space beneath the great trees littered with Grear corpses, a dying Human, and a short slender messenger. Stab wounds slid beneath scales marred the hide of four Grears. Charred marks obliterated the chests of five more. There was a short black stone rod at rest at the base of the hillside. The stone rod bore vertical quartz stripes at the tip running the length past the center before the rod became black stone again.

The black blood of the Grears withered the grass around them. Var laid his head back against the hill. His sight was fading. He thought he might live long enough to hear this letter before the numbing affect the wound was having on his limbs passed through the rest of his body and he passed from this life into higher halls. After tearing the Grear's bladed tail out from between the black plates of his own armor and flinging it onto the grass he did not feel the need to move from his own indentation in the dirt. His thoughts were spinning. The ache in his head from the thrashing blow to his helm did not make him want to listen to her words, but listen he did.

"To Var Al'keel, First Knight of the Stone Keep, keeper of the Lady Talleria's magic metal, wielder of the mighty blade, Dragon Tail Cleaver, and holder of the great Sage Stone Rod of Hadelhar. Greetings from his Majesty...."

"Skip the title," said Var Al'keel growling the words.

"Wouldn't you like to know who the king that is addressing you is?" she asked.

"Child," said Var placing his hand back over the fingers on his other hand pressed against the wound that was leaking blood. "When you are as old as me, and you do not have long to live. You do not much care what king sends such a small messenger who is not a healer, I might add, out to read him the letter while he is dying without sending a detachment of troops to finish the job."

The child shrugged, the ends of her long hair falling off her shoulders in a golden shower. The weary knight confused her locks with the sunlight shining on a waterfall he remembered from his youth. Then the memory was gone when she continued reading.

"You are hereby ordered to return home. The war with the Grear is over. The truce struck on the night of No Moon in the Year of the Flying Badgers with the King of the Grear has brought the war to an end. And, as such, your mission to assassinate the King of the Grear would grievously affect the peace of the Kingdoms of Zaderin. This letter is wizard flamed to self-destruct after all the words are read and the nature of your mission must be forever buried in your memory. Signed, His Majesty…."

"NO TITLES!" Var growled through his teeth. "That son of the wolves can keep his truce. What lying slippery twisted snake of an adviser convinced him to make a truce with the Grear! They never keep their truces. I remember. Nine of my brother knights died defending our king when the last truce was broken by the same Grear King. Does he remember this? No, he is off drifting in a cloud with this feathered dream of a truce."

"Do you wish me to read the rest of the letter?" asked the messenger patiently.

"No, I do not," said the knight angrily losing his breath when he raised his head.

The Grear head on the grass beside them jerked up and forward from the body towards the Whistler, jaw gaping with sharp ivory teeth. The Grear was not fully dead but merely unconscious until now. The knight struck out with his fist and swung at the Grear's head faster than the Whistler could think but he missed. It was not his gauntlet that struck the Grear but the raised bladed fin on the arm of his plated armor. The blade pierced the Grear between the metallic scales and brought the attack to a stand still. The knight waved off the Whistler's thanks and shook off the Grear's dead head in the same motion with a stern grunt of pain.

"What I wish," said the knight, his voice went from a low whisper and became louder. "Is that the king had sent knights instead of a tiny child. How in the hell did you get this deep into Grear country on your own? Are you not with a group? Is there no healer? Answer me!"

"No healer," she said. "Your people call mine The Whistlers."

"A Whistler?" said Var and again he laid his head back against the hillside. "Come take my helm off Whistler and tell me of your race. They say your people leave their memories on the wind in places is that true?"

"Yes," she said tucking the letter away into the Sabertooth pouch, and moving around to lift the dented helmet off his head so that he might better hear her speak. She carefully stepped around the great sword coated with the black of Grear blood and sat down again in her original place setting the heavy helmet beside her. "On a good day you can hear the memories of my people for many dragon lengths across the plains. They echo in the hollows of the hills and travel faster than light across the waters and through the very air. We hear them in the wind."

"And what do the whistles echoing in this place say? Said the knight, turning his head painfully to watch her sitting in a pool of sunlight.

She frowned and a wrinkle appeared in her bright brow. "In this place a family of Whistlers were killed by the Grear many years ago on the day the Grear invaded this land. It was before you were born if I've measured Human years aright, but after the great rains that made the deserts into the swamps."

"Does that not make you want to punish them for what they have done?"

"No," she said. "Of what use would that be? They kill your people. You kill theirs and it goes on until there are no people left. That is not revenge. That is self inflicted hurt that will last for centuries and it does nothing to help your children."

"How did you know I have children?"

"There are nine dead Grear," She said simply. "There are no other soldiers with you. A man who fights so fiercely is either senselessly mad or he must have a great need to return home."

The pain of his own laughter was almost too hard to bear and his sight went black for a moment before he could speak. "And you do not think I am mad."

"You do not speak like a madman," she said taking out her knife and cutting a strip of leather from her cloak. "So you must have children that you love enough to protect."

"Three," he said but he did not say their names, his breath was labored now and his lungs were heavy with a dark weight.

It was then that the earth trembled with a great echoing thud and then a second and a third until the knight thought the mountain was coming down in a great landslide. His lungs expanded enough to bring in air and he opened eyes he did not remember having shut.

"Oh, good," said the Whistler. "The healer is here."

"Healer?" said the knight, voice low and losing volume. "But there is not a healer, not for miles and miles, none west of the last town."

"No. Not a Human healer," said Whistler. "But who said a Human healer would ever answer the call of a whistler. Humans cannot even hear our whistling in the higher ranges."

"Then who answered?" said the knight but before he could say another word he coughed and fell unconscious back against the turf. That was perhaps for the best thought the Whistler watching the enormous being thunder down the path.

"Good morning, Grimba," said the Whistler.

Grimba roared her greeting scaring any of the remaining wildlife in the area, and then grunted in disapproval for being summoned so early in the morning. Green skin and knobby protrusions lined her great head. Lanky moss covered her head at the top and back, or it might have been hair. The Whistler was not sure, and she was too polite to ask a Troll.

"It is this knight here. I cannot deliver the letters to him if he is dead and well he is dying and I cannot lift the Grear off him so I thought maybe you could, especially since I have a message for you, too, from your husband Mabu Mabu and from your son Mabrimba."

Grimba made a small, disgruntled growl when she saw the state of the Human knight. Then she tossed the Grear carcass that lay across the knight completely off the hill. It landed several feet into the steep side of the mountain below the meadow at the base of the hill causing a rockslide. When the Whistler gave the Troll a stern glance, Grimba simply shrugged.

"Is Hy Las here?" asked the Whistler.

Grimba gave a low growl in response. Hy Las, the barbarian, was not in the mountains but a higher pitched whistle might find her on the plains near the mountains. After prying off a few of the smaller plates, not spiked or bladed, in the knight's armor she made the disappointing conclusion that he should not be moved but he was not dead yet.

The Whistler wandered off to the base of the hill after giving off a higher whistle. Grimba was pulling healing lichens and herbs from her hide bag and applying them to the swollen areas on the knight's flesh. She tucked a few leaves under the knight's armor nearer the wound. She dared not pry the knight's armor completely off the wound. It was the armor and the cloth beneath that kept the blood from gushing out of his body at a rate that she feared would be beyond her skills to heal. She gave another low growl that only the Whistler understood.

"It is not a written letter," she said. "Mabrimba sends his regards and requests a meeting with his mother the great Troll Healer."

Grimba growled again and tossed another Grear corpse more gently to the side. She ripped out a smaller tree in thoughts of making a travois. Whistler noticed the light glinting on the stripes of clear, white in the black stone rod at the base of the hill. She knelt down and picked it up turning it around in her hands thoughtfully. The Troll growled that it was likely magic and should be left alone but the Whistler shrugged. Whistlers were immune to magic save the healing and none knew why this was save the Whistlers and they kept the secret of their race very close. Grimba gave a growl and in response the Whistler brought the stone rod of clear white stripes up the hill and set it in the Troll's giant hand. The Troll set it atop the armor and growled a few words that made the rod shine with light.

"I did not know the Sage Stone Rod of Hadelhar could heal," said the Whistler and then replied to the growls Grimba let out and the rustling sounds she heard. "He did not know either? But it was his wasn't it? I mean how come only healers know the words to unlock the healing? Shouldn't the knight be able to use it too? Oh, you think that rule is stupid too. I wasn't blaming you, Grimba. I know you did not make the artifact. What is that noise?"

Springing out onto the hill rushed a great huge Grear long black claws extended to their full wicked sharp lengths headed towards the knight. The landing was a sharp clang for the knight's armor had more than enough sharp edges to strike the Grear's own spiked hide. Hearing the noise the Troll turned around and struck the Grear over the head with her club. The Grear fell against the knight and the Troll knelt down to lift the Grear off flinging the dead corpse to the side. She let off a mournful growl over her club. It was ruined by the sharp curve of the bladed fin jutting from the head of the Grear. The trapezoid space in the middle of the bladed fin caused greater damage and a shower of splinters from the club when the Troll snapped it away from the dead. She would have to make a new club.

"Hitting the Grear again?" said a male voice from the treeline.

"Shut Ruddy!" said the Whistler and ran up to the great barbarian who stood by the hill.

Clean-shaven, tall, and solid he was Hy Las's brother and the sole man among the barbarians emerging from the trees who did not have a beard. His reddish brown locks flung wide around when he lifted the Whistler, twirled her around in the air, and set her back onto her feet.

"What a reception you have received," said the woman who was much shorter than her brother but her hair was no less long for they had been traveling in the wild lands for many years.

"Hy Las!" said the Whistler and gave her a welcoming hug that the barbarian woman returned.

"Still walking about in that jacket and clothing I made from that shed hide of a Sabortooth that you found in the mountains, I see," said Rugana, the oldest woman of the barbarians who stood near the trees.

"And thanks again," said the Whistler. "Your son in the city of Beren bids you greeting and says that though he finds the ways of the city people strange, their ways are well worth learning."

"I thought you had a message for me, also," said Hy Las laughing.

"Yes," said the Whistler. "The man who wants to be a brother-in-law wishes you well. He bids you to continue to carry the ring for your sister until you have found her or he has found her. And if you should find her before him then to give her the ring as you have already agreed so that he and she may be betrothed though they are yet far apart. He still wishes to marry her but he has not found her yet."

"Alas for our sister," said Shut Ruddy laughing. "I still do not approve the marriage between them."

"And she left because of you," said Hy Las. "Had you not forbidden their marriage she would not have run off as she did to be with him, and we would know where she is right now."

"I find a single comfort in that he does not know where she is either!" said Shut Ruddy bringing a great deal of laughter from all of the barbarians save Hy Las who placed a hand on her sword.

"Be relieved my son," said Ruganna. "That it was Shilias who you forbade to marry, for had it been Hy Las I do believe you would have had a duel on your hands."

"Oh, and you believe Hy Las would have married a dueling man?"

"Nay, my son," said Rugana. " I do believe she would have dueled you herself for his hand."

This brought greater laughter to the barbarians. The knight awoke at the ruckus and stared about himself with wide eyes for never had he witnessed the gathering of a Troll, a Whistler, and a company of barbarians all together in the same space. The Whistler immediately went to his side and knelt down to speak with him about her friends.

"Don't worry," said the Whistler to the knight who could hardly move for the razor metal set in his armor was embedded in the turf of the hillside. "This is Grimba the healer and she figured out that the Sage Stone Rod of Hadelhar you've been carrying around has healing properties when in direct contact with the magic metal of your armor. And this is Hy Las, Shut Ruddy, Rugana, and their friends. They are barbarians but you do not need to fear them because they are survivors from the Darian clan and they fought on your side during the war."

"It explains why you speak more like the Beren city dwellers than the barbarian tribes that used to roam the plains," said the knight. "But what brings you so far into Grear country?"

"And why not?" said Shut Ruddy. "Our tribes have been destroyed and scattered to the wind so we shall wander where the wind goes forevermore. There are no closed borders to us now. We, who have faced death all day and night long, fear no race and no thing made by man or evil spirit. This is our world. Shall we not raise our families wherever we choose."

"But to bring children into the land of the Grear?" said the knight.

"There is no safe place for us now, so we go everywhere. Our families will be everywhere." Said Rugana. "Everyone is our tribe now. There is no reassurance that your country will not fall to the Grear or the Grear country fall to yours. So we place our families on all continents in all countries. We are the family who chose the land the Grear now hold and whether we perish or stand strong we know our family survives. In this way we win all wars."

"There is a benefit to living in the Grear country," said Shut Ruddy beating a place on his great cloak coated with dust. "Here we do not have to hide who we are. If they find us they kill us so we can carry our weapons in the open instead of hidden."

Grimba growled and the Whistler translated. "Grimba does not think much of your city dwellers. She thinks more of the barbarians. She says they are the people of the mountains."

"People of the mountains," laughed the knight painfully. "But if you never build castles and great halls to live in, you'll always be confined to survival instead of being given the chance to learn the greater arts."

"Nay," said Rugana. "For when a child of our race has a desire to learn an art we send the child and an older guardian to travel to the place where the best teachers are. In this way many of our people are masters whereas yours are confined by the idea that they must only live up to the status assigned them instead of becoming more for their people."

"But your people are poor." Var said. "You have no wealth to pay for the teaching of your children."

"We find a way to trade for their teaching if the master of the art will not accept our children to be an apprentice," said Shut Ruddy. "I myself fought against a gladiator in the arena in exchange for my younger brother's apprenticeship with a shipwright. I still can't believe he wanted to build ships! What more does a man need than an honest sword in his hand?"

"Intelligence?" said Hy Las and her brother leapt off the rock he was standing on to come around and swat at her with an empty hand. She quickly countered by drawing her dagger and he backed away without ever having delivered the swat.

"Remember. Your sister is smaller than you." said Rugana. "And there be more than one man here who would defend her were you to have a true scuffle."

"It is I who should be defending her against them," said Shut Ruddy glaring at the few men who had taken a step when he had raised his hand.

Grimba roared and Rugana translated. "Settle down. We have no need for fighting. It appears this brave knight of Beren is wounded."

"There is a cave in the hills, not far from here."

"Yes," said Rugana. "I highly doubt we can take him to the home of the Troll healer. The cave it is."

Very carefully they began to unbind his armor but he stopped them all and insisted he could walk provided someone strong enough could lift him to his feet. Grabbing onto the places on his armor that had no upraised sharp edges Grimba lifted the knight out of the turf and onto his feet.

"Come." Said Hy Las and the barbarians helped the knight up the hill around the rocks and into the cave oblivious of the Grear who watched from behind a downfallen log on the other side of the hill. The rest of the healing took many hours until dusk swept down over the entrance of the cave and the barbarians brought out their own means of light.

The knight reluctantly allowed them to remove plates on his armor to allow the Troll healer to peer at his wounds. The gravest injury was no more than a white scar sealed over by the Sage Rod the Troll had set over the knight's armor. The barbarians bound the rest of his smaller hurts up with clean cloths they saved for wrapping wounds.

"Grimba says she will teach you the words," said the Whistler, when the Troll was finished healing the knight and laid the Sage Rod into his gauntlet. "So you can become a healer knight and heal yourself when you need too."

"That would be a relief," said Var Al'keel with a grunt of pain when a barbarian child pulled a bandaging cloth too tight.

"The words are the same no matter what the language," said the Whistler. "So you won't have to do any growling."

"Thanks," said the knight.

"It is we who should be thanking you," said Shut Ruddy. "It was your presence that let us know there were Grear in the area. Our scouts just killed two that were hiding near the cave."

"Your people kill Grear?" said the Knight. "But you wear no armor."

Shut Ruddy laughed. "Perhaps that makes our people braver. No, most of the time we bribe them to leave us alone but when we cannot then we use stones."

"Stones?" said the knight touching the hilt of his great magic sword Hy Las had brought up into the cave from the hill.

"Every creature has a sensitive place. A Grear's is right below the jaw. They do not lift their heads often but if you can make a noise above them on the hill they will and then you hit them with a stone."

"And that is your way of survival?" said the knight. "No armies."

"No armies," said Shut Ruddy. "They studied how to destroy armies. We live. The Dimthal died because they tried to fight the Grear with armies. Live among all races respecting their ways but keeping to your own, without fighting when possible, and your people will win, but to hold to a certain parcel of land is foolishness. What if the land goes bad or it is overrun by war?"

"Or overrun by Trolls?" Shut Ruddy grinned bringing out a metal cup to pour in the content from the wineskin he carried about his shoulders.

Grimba growled. Shut Ruddy laughed and patted her on the shoulder. The Whistler sat down on a great hide they unrolled to cover the cave floor. It was warm. The floor was cold.

Shut Ruddy spoke again. "Grimba told me her people survived for centuries doing exactly this and why should not Humans survive for centuries doing the same? When all of your mighty cities have fallen we will still be here. Not Trolls, Grear, or any other race will be able to wipe Humans from the earth. They might take the cities but not us. The survival of the Human race is what we barbarians are."

"Grimba says the wolves, the antelope, the deer, even the smallest of creatures understand this secret to life." The Troll growled and the Whistler translated what the Troll spoke. "Yet your people will not survive if they do not understand this."

The knight grunted again when the barbarian child pulled another bandage too tight but loosened it quickly when he gave the child a stern look. "I thank you for your words of wisdom, Grimba, but our city still stands."

"And we will keep it that way," said Shut Ruddy finishing the knight's sentence before he could speak. "So spoke the chiefs of our clan. You might notice there are no more chiefs of our clans. We are families scattered across the lands carrying the pride of our people and in saving our families we have great pride."

Rugana sat down beside a child Var knew was not of the barbarian tribe for the color of his hair and his looks did not match.

"And we take pride in saving the children of those who have died regardless of their race and raising them, also, as our own. This child's parents were killed by the Grear. We now are stronger by a single child, and who knows what this child will do when grown. Perhaps here is the next greatest healer or the newest painter, a masterful smith, or the best warrior of them all. We shall be pleased whatever this child chooses."

"But you are far from the great cities," said the knight. "How will you know if this child is destined to be a painter or a smith? You have nothing of a painter's work or a smith's out here in the wild."

"The smallest child knows," said Rugana rummaging through their backpacks and supplies to make sure they had more bandages. "Is there not art in the wild lands? Is there not a campfire and metalwork here in the wildlands? We shall know by what he does. Did not my smallest daughter blend together berries and spread it across the hide of my cloak making this splotch? And did she stop when I told her to. No. She continued to paint though none of us showed her the way all through her days in the wild lands. She asked to become a painter and was apprenticed in Beren where another of my sons watches over her."

"But you must admit," said the knight. "Not all children can become painters or who would run the cities and cook for the soldiers?"

"Have more children," said Rugana in her quavering old voice. "There are many people who enjoy cooking and administrating. But I dare say these talents are harder to discover than painting."

"Aye, drink to that!" shout Shut Ruddy who held his wife close to him, winked at his sister, and raised his glass in toast to his mother's words. "And when, Hy Las, will you be having children?"

"Not today, I think," said Hy Las laughing. She had chosen no one and no man had chosen her making it nigh impossible for any children to be in her future. "But for you and your lady I think it will be soon."

"Aye, to Dilisa!" he said, and drank to his wife and many of the men drank with him but Hy Las did not drink. "So, shall we waste good barbarian wine on this knight from Beren?"

Shut Ruddy brought forth his wineskin and gave it to the knight who drank from it and to his surprise found that it held no alcohol. He laughed after taking a drink. "Your lot is too clear headed for me."

"And yet you call us the barbarians!" said Shut Ruddy.

The barbarian who rushed into the cave carrying a spear did not join in their laughter. His speech was for Shut, Hy Las, and Rugana, but the knight was close enough to hear what they said.

"They have returned," said the barbarian in low tones. "The Grear hold council outside the white rocks near the cave. We must be silent and cease our movements."

"Nay," said Rugana. "For if they are there then they have already found us. Let us continue on laughing and drinking. We shall send our best to listen to their talk and determine what they intend to do. It may be that they are only passing by us and if not, perhaps they can be bribed or silenced."

"If they are to be silenced," said the knight. "Then I would go with you."

"They do not hear the way that we do so you may keep your armor," said Rugana picking up her walking staff. "But you must stay behind the rocks. For they sense movement and only our scouts understand how to move so that they think us only animals."

Quickly they choose who would stay and who would go. Grimba chose to remain behind, busy at work carving a new club from a tree she had brought with her on the hike to the cave. She said she would not come until she was finished reinforcing the club.

Hy Las, Shut, a few more of the barbarians, the knight, and the Whistler crept through the darkness outside the cave down to stand behind the rocks. The Whistler who knew all languages soon began to translate the clicking sounds she heard the Grear making. Several of the barbarian scouts remained in their positions surrounding the Grear but to fight this many of the six clawed beings seemed too much for the barbarians at hand.

"It is their king," said the Whistler. "He says he wants to break the truce his son has made with the Humans and invade their land but his son is arguing with him. His son wants their people to migrate to the great glaciers. He says they made an ancient promise to colonize the land of the great glaciers to his great grandfather."

"Great," said Shut. "And did they happen to mention a bunch of Humans up in a cave?"

"Not so far," said the Whistler.

"What do you want to do?" asked Rugana of the knight who was holding the handle of the Sage Rod in a clenched fist. "This concerns all Humans."

"I would fight them," said the knight. "But if I do then they will say we broke the truce though it is they who speak of it."

"Then we wait," said Rugana. "With such hot heads it shall not be long before there is battle."

"The Old King of the Grear is saying that his son is weak and that if he will not go to war with the Humans then he should die here and now." Translated the Whistler.

There was a great racket of metal, loud clicks, and the scrap of many scales. The knight peered around the rock and witnessed many Grear setting upon a single Grear who held his own flinging his sharp tail about him to keep his space. The old king was missing the trapezoid razor fin on his head and wore instead a helm of spikes.

The knight raised the Sage Rod and shot the old king with a lightning strike. Then he quickly set upon each of the Grear attacking the lone Grear using lightning strikes from the Sage Rod. All were startled. The barbarians and the Whistler faded back into the night hiding in places were they could throw stones. Hy Las, Rugana, and Shut stood near the knight. The knight handed the Sage Rod to Rugana and she continued shooting the Grear with the rods of lightning. He rushed in with his bladed armor drawing his great sword to do battle with the king of the Grear.

Rugana said to Hy Las and Shut, who wisely remained out of the line of lightning strikes. "Even if he kills the old king the younger might decide that this is Human treachery and choose to avenge his father instead of taking his people to explore the great glaciers."

"Yeah," said Shut. "But I'll never get a chance to watch a battle between a Beren Knight and the King of the Grear again."

The tail of a Grear embedded itself into the rock near all three and Shut cleaved the tail off before Rugana shot the offending Grear. Hy Las and Shut cleaved off anything that threatened Rugana from that minute on and when they weren't busy defending her they were making comments on the fight between Var Al'keel and the Grear King.

The Grear King was swinging his bladed tail at the knight's armor but had not yet learned the knack of sliding it beneath the knight's chest plates. The knight had cinched the straps holding his plate armor on too tightly for the Grear to slide a bladed tail beneath them but not too tight to be able to move. Twice the length of a tall Human with six legs the last two near the tail built longer and stronger, the Grear was more limber and faster.

The Grear King used this to his advantage by keeping his distance. Var relentlessly closed this distance between them, rapidly swinging his great sword at the Grear King, but the king kept retreating too quickly to be killed. Then the Grear King's tail struck a huge tree and his head whipped around to find out why he could not free his tail from the trunk. Having many bladed clawed limbs is a great advantage in a battle but the negative side to this is keeping track of all of them so they do not hit what they are not supposed to. With the Grear King's mobility limited the knight charged forward, not too quickly that he could not swing to the right or to the left, but with enough force to drive his sword through the Grear's scaled body. The advantage to being smaller than a Grear is near the same of being a small stone in a sling aimed at a pole. The target is slightly bigger.

The son of the Grear King was entangled with two other Grear struggling to slash up under their scales. The barbarian scout and the Whistler brought down the outermost Grear. When Grimba waded in there could be no doubt whose side would win the battle but it did mean that Grimba was going to have to make another club.

When all was said and slashed there lay on the ground Grear corpses dead from rocks, Grear dead with the combined force of a Troll's club, blades, and lightning, and two dying of Grear bladed wounds including the son of the Grear King, and the knight was wounded again. Grimba shook her head. The barbarians quickly laid the knight down and placed the Sage Rod on his chest plate and

Grimba taught him the words with the Whistler's help to begin his healing. Among the Grear crawling away from his assailants the son of the king bled black blood from many wounds. He clicked and the Whistler translated for him. His bright diamond reflective eyes fixed on the barbarians.

"Are you assassins sent from the Humans to kill the king?" asked the young Grear. "Was my father right? Are the Humans not to be trusted?"

"We are barbarians from the North," said Hy Las. "We honor your truce and so does the knight who lays here on the ground but we could not stand by while your Royal Highness was killed. We acted to protect your life."

The Whistler picked up two white stones. She translated the words spoken aloud back to the Grear with the stones. Striking them together in her hands she carefully made the clicking noises of his race.

The young Grear brought his long scaly neck back at this thought but his diamond eyes gleamed. The grass was slicked black with his blood but he managed to crawl forward on all six clawed limbs to where the knight was and peer at him. He clicked again and the Whistler translated.

"Beren steal idea for armor from us. Did you know we forged the Sage Rod and gave it to the Humans centuries ago at Hadelhar when they joined with us to fight the Trolls?"

There was more clicking but the Whistler stopped translating and all looked to her. She shrugged. Then she shook her head.

"I think he is laughing," said the Whistler but then Grimba growled and the Whistler had more to translate. "Grimba, says that if the Grear do not leave soon, then the Trolls are planning a revolt and I can tell you what she says is true I carry two messages to her asking her to join their army."

The young Grear's head wove back and forth between the Humans, the Whistler, and the Troll. More clicking sounded from the inner square teeth housed behind the sharp curved fangs. The Whistler again translated.

"He says he will take his people to the glaciers to fulfill his promise to his grandfather. He says his race alone is suited to carving off blocks of ice and shipping it to the Southern lands so that the races may be cooled by it. The Grear have trade agreements with the Dwarves and have helped them forge weapons for centuries so they will find a way to keep the ice cool enough to ship south. His race are not afraid of volcanoes and ice so why should they live in the softer lands and make war on the weaker people."

Grimba growled and the Whistler translated. "Grimba says if you will not make war on the Trolls then she would place herbs on you to make you well enough to return to your people, but she says she will not heal your enemy Grear."

The other dying Grear sliced at the son of the king with his sharp tail but the Troll caught the tail and pulled the Grear up by it swinging it around and around until the Grear's head struck the rock and smeared it with black blood. So died the last of the old Grear king's guards.

The young Grear allowed Grimba to take the herbs from her bag and place them on his wounds. When the knight was nearly healed she borrowed one of the knight's gauntlets and used the Stone Rod of Hadelhar upon the young Grear. When he was healed he rose to his two hind legs shook claws with the great healer Troll. Var the knight said not a thing until the Grear had gone back into the darkness.

"Grimba, you are wiser than I thought a Troll could ever be," admitted Var slowly when he sat up and rested his forearms on the guards of his sword that was still embedded in the corpse of the old King of the Grear.

Grimba growled and the Whistler translated. "Wisdom comes from being a parent, not from being a Troll."

Thus did the Grear leave on their great adventure to settle the glaciers at the tip of the world. The knight returned to his family. Grimba put a halt to the Troll rebellion. The barbarians continued traveling on their way, and the Whistler stood that night upon a hillside and whistled this tale into the wind.

www.ingramcontent.com/pod-product-compliance
Lightning Source LLC
Chambersburg PA
CBHW020644130626
46552CB00003B/1396